The
Smithsonian
Collection

D1528130

· Old Time Radio ·

# MYSTERIES

**by**
**Lawrence Nepodahl**

**Foreword by**
**David Kogan**

David Kogan

# Foreword

I became hooked on radio at a very early age. The year was 1930, to be exact. With a few dollars savings, I purchased a crystal set and a pair of earphones. It was late at night, when reception was best, that I came upon one of the earliest radio dramas. It was a show titled *The First Nighter Program*. As a youngster, I lay in my bed in the dark, magically transported to "The Little Theatre Off Times Square." Mr. First Nighter, our host of the program, guided us through the traffic of Broadway. Horns were blowing, people talking, the sound of police whistles. All street noises faded as the genial Mr. First Nighter led us into the theatre. There was only the murmur of the expectant audience. The curtain went up and the play began.

I was completely captivated by radio, as were millions of other Americans. The year 1930 was the beginning of the Great Depression. With growing unemployment and hard times, most people were bound to their homes. Radio provided free entertainment, and the thirties were the beginning of the Golden Age of Radio. Heightened by music and sound effects, radio drama held listeners enthralled.

The power of radio on imagination was never more revealing than on the night of October 30, 1938, when Orson Welles' Martian invasion broadcast of "The War of the Worlds" had thousands of frightened listeners flooding police switchboards with frantic calls. A great number of them fled their homes, intent on escaping the invaders. It was imagination run wild.

I began writing for radio as a freelance writer in the late thirties. I wrote for programs such as *The Shadow*, *The Thin Man* and *Bulldog Drummond*.

In 1940 I met a fellow writer, Bob Arthur. We became collaborators with a view to creating and producing our own radio packages, and hopefully selling one to a network.

Our first effort was a dramatic program that we titled, *The Mysterious Traveler*. Each broadcast would be a complete thirty-minute story in the field of mystery. The signature of the program was the wail of a locomotive whistle in the distance. As the oncoming train comes on full, we are in the club car with The Mysterious Traveler, who is our host. Above the sound of the train, he greets us, and leads us into the story of the evening.

The final scene and the climax of the story bring the listener back to the club car and the whistle of the speeding train. The Mysterious Traveler sardonically comments on the evening's story, and regrets having to see you leave the train.

We presented the package to the Mutual Broadcasting System, and contracted with Mutual to write, direct and produce *The Mysterious Traveler* on a weekly basis.

Mutual was to provide the broadcast studio, the engineer, soundman, organist and announcer. We in turn produced the show, providing script, cast and direction. Our contract gave us complete freedom as to the themes and contents of our scripts.

In the nine years that followed, and in some four hundred and fifty scripts we wrote, Bob and I roamed widely in every realm of drama: Horror, Fantasy, Supernatural, Science Fiction, Suspense.

As collaborators, we spent one day a week bouncing ideas off each other in our pursuit of a theme and a plot for a script. I would be seated at a desk with a writing pad and paper, while Bob would be stretched out on a couch. Quite often he would drift off to sleep. Invariably he would awaken from his catnap with a start, and ask, "Where are we?"

When we arrived at a complete story outline, one or the other would write the dialogue for the script. I served as director of *The Mysterious Traveler*, Bob as producer. The freedom we were given as to script themes was almost unique in the field of radio. Only Arch Oboler, with his *Lights Out* program, was given such a free hand.

During our nine-year run, we cast scores of actors and actresses on our show. Those we cast were all experienced and talented, able to seize upon a role with very little direction. A number of them went on to Hollywood and films: Art

Carney, Shirley Booth, Jeff Chandler, Jessica Tandy and Eva Marie Saint were but a few.

A day of broadcast would begin with the cast and myself gathered around a studio table. Scripts would be passed out and there would be the initial reading. A first-time reading followed this on mike, with our engineer and myself in the control booth. Then came a second run-through with sound and music integrated. During this run there would be frequent pauses for level settings, reading interpretations and balances between sound and music. After a short break, our announcer would put in an appearance and we would do a full dress rehearsal with a timing of the show. If the program ran over the allotted twenty-nine minutes and thirty seconds of airtime, I would make the necessary script cuts so that we ended exactly on time.

Of great interest to us was the mail we received from our listeners. This mail was unsolicited. Most weekly broadcasts brought in from twenty to thirty pieces of mail, coming from all regions of the country. Comments on the show would run from approval, disbelief, queries as to plot, and requests for a photo of Maurice Tarplin, who played the role of The Mysterious Traveler for the nine years we were on the air.

Now and then our listeners would be so caught up with a show, that it would bring forth an avalanche of mail. A program titled "Full Fathom Fifty" brought in over three hundred pieces of mail. The script was written in the final weeks of

World War II. The world was waiting at that time for the capture of Adolf Hitler. Our script had Hitler on a submarine, making his escape to Argentina. A very fine actor, Lon Clark, played the role of Hitler, and his impersonation of Hitler was letter-perfect. The submarine, making its way submerged deep in the Atlantic, had Hitler and his party becoming aware of what seemed to be scratching sounds on the hull of the submarine. A member of Hitler's party panics at the ever-mounting sound, convinced the scratching on the hull is being made by the drowned victims of Hitler's navy. Hysteria sets in, with Hitler being the shrillest of the lot. Hitler orders the captain to surface, despite the possibility of discovery. The captain at first resists the order, but finally gives in to Hitler's screams. He orders that the ballast tanks be pumped out. As the scratching intensifies, Hitler demands to know why the submarine is not rising. The captain is baffled. The ballast tanks have been completely emptied, yet the sub hasn't risen at all. To the contrary, it is slowly going deeper. A member of the party screams that it is the dead outside the hull who are taking them down. Panic ensues, with Hitler screaming threats to the captain. Rivets begin to pop, hull plates weaken, the submarine sinks deeper and deeper. Among the cries and screams, Hitler's hysteria rises above all. The water comes rushing in.

Almost all the letters expressed delight at Hitler's end, and there were many letters asking for a repeat of the show.

A show that drew an equal amount of mail was titled, "The Last Survivor." Written in 1949, long before the Russians sent Sputnik into space, and long before we began our own space program, it was pure science fiction. It dealt with an American spaceship returning from the moon, and circling Earth in preparation for a landing. Suddenly the crew becomes aware of huge explosions taking place on Earth. Nuclear warfare has broken out. As they watch in disbelief and horror, a huge blast emanating from Earth reaches their spaceship and severely damages it. They find their spaceship inoperable, due to the blast. Slowly the realization comes to them that they are destined to wander in space until they die.

I still recall the memorable scripts of half a century ago, but with those pleasant memories come the unforgettable mishaps that occurred while we were on the air.

There was the show where our lead actor, seeking revenge, declared his intention to shoot his enemy. Our soundman, on cue, fires his gun. Not a sound was heard. A second quick pull of the trigger by the soundman, but no shot rang out. Our quick-witted actor, noting the gun failure, cried out, "Shooting is too good for you! This knife should do it!" A fierce lunge, a grunt, and the soundman comes in with a heavy body fall. Music up sharply. A salute to the quick-witted actor.

But then there was the mishap of all mishaps. In this particular show, our hero, who was recently married to a beautiful and mysterious woman, finds that those near and dear to him are meeting unexplainable deaths. In the final scene he comes to realize that he has married a witch, and that it is she who has been destroying those he loves. This revelation, and her taunts, drive him into a towering rage. He seizes her by the throat and starts choking her. The script called for him to furiously utter, "Die! Witch! Die!" Unfortunately, in the heat of the moment, the uttered line came out, "Die! Bitch! Die!" For a brief moment everyone in the studio stared at the actor in disbelief. Mercifully the soundman did the call for a body fall. A dramatic organ crescendo gave way to the locomotive whistle and the speeding train. The Mysterious Traveler sardonically dwelt on the risks in marrying a beautiful stranger.

Of the mail that we received on that show, only four objected to the language. It was our feeling that most listeners couldn't believe their ears.

Looking back, a half century later, I can't think of anything else I might have engaged in that would have been as interesting.

*David Kogan*

The sound effects wizards do their best to create the compelling sounds of mystery.

# There Is Mystery on the Airwaves

The slow sinister creaking of a door . . . the forlorn wailing of a train . . . the ominous ticking of a clock: these are some of the sounds of mystery. "It . . ., is . . ., later . . ., than . . ., you . . ., thiiinnnk." "Yes, I know the nameless terrors of which they dare not speak." "Want to get away from it all?" These are some of the words of mystery. These particular words and sounds made for edge-of-your-chair entertainment during the Golden Age of Radio.

The mystery story is one of the most compelling and well-received forms of creative expression. The mystery story by definition means any affair, thing or person that presents features or points so obscure as to arouse curiosity or speculation. Its true history can be traced back to the bible so why wouldn't this singular genre lend itself quite well to the radio medium?

The classifications of the mystery drama are similar to the Hydra of Greek mythology. Multi-headed, but sharing the same heart, there are several categories and subcategories within the mystery genre: the detective has the "gentleman" or "tough guy," the crime has the "police procedural," the thriller has "supernatural horror," and the historical has "Gothic" content or some other century idea the author creates. The mystery genre also ventured into the spy and juvenile subcategories. All these embodiments were covered on radio: the detective mystery, *Ellery Queen*; *Sherlock Holmes*; the crime mystery, *Gangbusters*; *This Is Your FBI*; the thriller mystery, *The Clock*; *Suspense*; the historical mystery, *The Weird Circle*; *Crime Classics*; the juvenile mystery, *Dick Tracy*; *Captain Midnight*; and the spy, *The Man Called X*; *Dangerous Assignment*.

The strength of the mystery drama was twofold: it was relatively economical to produce and it was attractive to the listening audience. Mystery series were much less costly than the comedy and musical programs, which abounded in radio. Performers such as Eddie Cantor and Al Jolson received lavish contracts before agreeing to step before the microphone. However, the mystery drama did not necessarily need expensive name actors or actresses—it just needed actors who had clear and distinctive voices and the ability to make their characters sound realistic.

This was not to say that the creators of radio mystery programs were so stingy they ignored big-name talent. *Sherlock Holmes* was one of the first programs to open its wallets to a well-known star . . . Basil Rathbone. *Suspense* was another high-profile mystery series that caught the attention of many celebrities. Right from the start, the on-air audition for *Suspense* boasted Herbert Marshall as the featured player in Marie Belloc Lowndes' noted story, "The Lodger." Topnotch film stars loved to work on *Suspense*. Cary Grant was quoted as saying in 1943, "If I ever do any more radio work, I want to do it on *Suspense*, where I get a good chance to act." Grant's wish was granted on many occasions including two with the scripts of the now popular mystery writer, Cornell Woolrich (a.k.a. William Irish) with "The Black Curtain" on November 30, 1944, and "The Black Path of Fear," on March 7, 1946.

Woolrich was a favorite scriptwriter for *Suspense* in its early years, as was John Dickson Carr (he wrote the first episode of *Suspense*, "The Burning Court"). "Cabin B-13" was Carr's most notable story — a woman is on her honeymoon and her husband disappears without leaving a trace that he ever existed. This captivating story was spun off into a mystery anthology of its own titled *Cabin B-13*. Debuting July 5, 1948, it starred Arnold Moss as Dr. Fabian who enjoyed spinning tales from Cabin B-13 on the luxury liner Maurevania.

Another mystery anthology series that had celebrities contending for an appearance was *Everyman's Theater*. Many of the stars (Joan Crawford, Charles Laughton) admired the work of the series' creator, Arch Oboler, and were eager to work with his genius. Later when television was becoming popular, network and agency producers lured Hollywood celebrities and mystery writers away from radio. In radio, Dick Powell starred as *Richard Diamond, Private Detective*, but during television's infancy, Powell produced a video version of his series starring newcomer David Janssen. Writers John Dickson Carr and Alfred Hitchcock hosted the radio series *Murder By Experts*, but had programs of their own on television.

In terms of entertainment, mystery programs afforded listeners the opportunity to either use their deductive powers, or just sit back and listen to a well-spun yarn. Certainly, mysteries entertained audiences and sold commercial products, but they also championed the simple pattern of right over wrong, good over evil and truth over lies. Whether it was a thriller or straight crime story, it engaged

The sound effects man was one of the most important ingredients to a mystery story.

the listeners' imaginations and transported them along an intense route toward a solution or conclusion to that mystery.

One of the most important ingredients to a mystery story was the sound effects man. He was the one who set the stage, painted the scenery, built the mood and provided the motif. When these realistic sound effects were combined with wonderful acting and writing, the result was truly a treat for the mind's eye. There definitely was mystery on the airwaves during the Golden Age of Radio, but there really wasn't any mystery to it . . . it was just fun!

Variety was the key to good mystery writing. It might be the key to the *Inner Sanctum*, or perhaps it opened the door to the office of *Sam Spade*. For the most part, *Nero Wolfe* never left his abode, letting his guy-Friday Archie Goodwin do his legwork, while *The Mysterious Traveler* went many places via an ominous train. *The Whistler* knew many strange things, for he walked by night, and *The Shadow* knew what evil lurked in the hearts of men. *Philip Marlowe* warned that crime was a suckers road, and those who traveled it would wind up in the gutter, the prison or the grave. Radio listeners could *Escape* for a half-hour of high adventure, or listen to tales well calculated to keep them in *Suspense*. But, if one frightened easily, it was advisable to turn the radio off and not listen to *Lights Out*. Yes, radio mystery was a multifaceted genre, sharing one heart of murder and mayhem; nonetheless, mystery could be found whatever direction the radio dial was turned in many a living room across America.

# THE PROGRAMS

Program notes by William Nadel and Lawrence Nepodahl
Cast identifications by William Nadel

**I.**

**THE CLOCK** 11/13/47: by Lawrence Klee. Larry White (producer); Clark Andrews (director); Glenn Osser (music); Terry Ross (sound effects). Starring Joe DeSantis (Eddie Evans); Alice Frost (Francine Moulton).

*A newspaper reporter falls for a wealthy widow recently acquitted of murder—but was she really innocent?*

The opening signature of this show (debut: November 3, 1946) voiced the motif: "Sunrise and sunset, promise and fulfillment, birth and death...the whole drama of life is written in the sands of time." The ticking of a timepiece along with the travel log type narration led the listener to believe that a pleasant and thoughtful tale was to follow ... an interesting direction for its writer Lawrence Klee to take. Klee was also the writer of another mystery/suspense program in which a unique introduction was used. On that series (*The Chase*), the introduction dealt with sounds of the hunt being heard. "The hunt of a man!" In addition, the melodramatic writing styling of Lawrence Klee could be

6

Joe DeSantis

heard on the radio detecting airwaves of *Mr. Keen, Tracer of Lost Persons* and *The Fat Man*, a.k.a. Brad Runyon.

Lawrence Klee's fame was such that days after his untimely death in the mid 1950s, the New York Public Library requested a collection of his scripts from his family. An Australian version of *The Clock* produced at that time which utilized Klee's original writing was so popular that it was even syndicated to American radio stations. Alice Frost, who is featured in this story (as the supposed femme fatale), had a most unusual and distinctive voice. Because of her vocalized diversity, she was a chosen favorite on many radio programs. Ten years before this outing, she took part in Orson Welles' ambitious undertaking of *Les Misérables* (available from Radio Spirits or your local bookstore). Broadcast in 1937, this classic Victor Hugo story of injustice and persecution hit the air a full year ahead of Welles' famous *Mercury Theatre on the Air* series. The sprawling novel was performed in seven half-hour installments from July 23 through September 3.

Ms. Frost also enjoyed success as one of the many soap opera queens of her day—performing on such soaps as *Big Sister*, *Bright Horizon*, *The Second Mrs. Burton* and *Woman of Courage*. She is probably best remembered, however, as wife Pam North to Joseph Curtin's Jerry, on the aptly titled *Mr. & Mrs. North*.

**2.**

disc 1
cass 1
side A/B

**ESCAPE** 03/20/49 "The Country of the Blind" by John Dunkel from the story by H. G. Wells. Norman Macdonnell (producer/director); Leith Stevens (music); William Conrad (Voice of *Escape*); Roy Rowan (announcer). Starring Edmond O'Brien (Nuñez); Berry Kroeger (Ybarra); Edgar Barrier (señor/doctor); Byron Kane (Pedro); Harry Bartell (Correa); Peggy Webber (Medina—sarote); Wilms Herbert (Yacob—the father).

*Falling into a strange valley of blind people, a man finds mysterious romance and fear.*

Much has been written about this anthology series (debut: July 7, 1947). Today it is widely considered one of radio's finest programs. Superb production values (even though it had a modest operating budget) make this and the other *Escape* episodes a pleasure to hear over and over again. It is a shame, that at the time, the show was not allowed to develop a faithful audience. It was shifted to at least eighteen different timeslots in its seven-year run. It was often used as a summer replacement, then dropped for weeks on end, only to turn up in different timeslots much later. Even its audition episode had an unusual history; it was produced on March 21, 1947, but the actual series did not start until four months later. Many of the *Escape* stories became radio classics and were later repeated on *Escape* and on its well-to-do sister series, *Suspense*. This particular script, adapted from H. G. Wells' story is just such an example.

Arch Oboler

## 3.

**EVERYMAN'S THEATER** 10/18/40 "Cat Wife" by Arch Oboler. Gordon Jenkins (music); Arch Oboler (director/host). Starring Raymond Edward Johnson (John); Betty Winkler (Linda); George Coulouris (doctor).

*Can a woman transform into a human-sized feline or is it just a strange trick of the imagination?*

The name Arch Oboler is synonymous with old time radio mystery and horror. Oboler liked to refer to his mysterious scripts as explorations into the supernormal and "Cat Wife" is one of his best. Writing of the mysterious/horrific came natural to Oboler. By the time he created *Everyman's Theater* (debut: October 4, 1940), he was already well-known for *Arch Oboler's Plays* and the famous *Lights Out* dramas.

*Everyman's Theater* was a blend of Oboler's dramas, originals and adaptations. The show exhibited the same craftsmanship that Oboler was famous for—unconventional plotting and stream-of-consciousness narration. "Cat Wife" was *Everyman's Theater*'s third broadcast. Its star, Raymond Edward Johnson, was an actor who took part in almost every station of radio. Everything from soap operas, *Brave Tomorrow* and *Valiant Lady*; science fiction, *Tales of Tomorrow* and *X Minus One*; crime/detective, *Gangbusters* and *Nick Carter, Master Detective*; and juvenile, *Don Winslow of the Navy* and *Tennessee Jed*. He played the title

Raymond Edward Johnson

character on *Mr. District Attorney* as well as *Roger Kilgore*, another public defender. He also took part in several anthology programs including Oboler's *Lights Out*. However, he is probably best known as Raymond, the sardonic host of *Inner Sanctum Mysteries*.

Mr. Johnson's costar in this story is Betty Winkler, a three-time winner of *Radio Mirror* magazine's readers' poll award as "Best Actress on the Air." Actors work best when they have worked with other actors before. They become accustomed to their fellow actors cadence of delivery. Such was the case with Johnson and Winkler; they had worked before on *Lights Out* and *Inner Sanctum*. Since Ms. Winkler had the most feline voice on radio, she is *perrrrrfect* for this story.

Winkler was said to have the sweetest voice on the airwaves so it was only natural that she should lend it to such soap operas as *Joyce Jordan M.D.* and *Girl Alone*, where a pleasant, soothing voice was obligatory. Her other radio work included *Don Winslow of the Navy*, *Lights Out*, *Curtain Time*, *The Chicago Theatre of the Air* and *Grand Hotel* (she was the switch board operator who connected the calls which would lead to that week's particular romantic story).

At one point, Winkler portrayed several of the female roles on *Fibber McGee & Molly* including Daisy, Dimples LaRue, Miss Fiditch, and Flossie. After her retirement from the acting profession, Ms. Winkler became

13

very active in the field of psychiatry, working as a therapist, and authored several books on the subject.

"Cat Wife" is an example of Oboler reusing a script that was performed before. It was heard two years earlier on his famous *Lights Out* series. On that night (April 6, 1938), its star was Boris Karloff, who was enjoying great fame having played the monster in Universal's smash hit *Frankenstein*.

**4.**

disc 2
cass 2
side A

**INNER SANCTUM MYSTERIES** 09/18/45 "Terror By Night" by Emile Tepperman. Himan Brown (producer/director); Mary Bennett (Lipton Tea spokeswoman). Starring Paul McGrath (host); Ann Shepherd (Linda Dickson); Santos Ortega (Dr. Roger Brice/radio voice); Luis Van Rooten (Joe Nesbitt/John Taylor).

*A woman, on her vacation, gets a lift from a man who just might be an escaped murder convict.*

"Good evening friends. This is your host, welcoming you in through the squeaking door to the Inner Sanctum." Each week, the ghoulish host, and the squeaking door were classic moments in radio broadcasting. Campy perhaps, but the series that grew out of it would be remembered decades after radio itself ceased to be dramatically viable. The brainchild of this well-conceived gimmick was its

Santos Ortega

Paul McGrath

creator/producer/director, Himan Brown. Brown explained the squeaking door genesis: "The studio door to the basement gave off an ungodly creak whenever anyone opened it. One day I thought to myself—I'm going to make that door a star."

Brown, like Arch Oboler, knew how to use the stuff of radio—producing just the right sounds of murder and mayhem. Even the organ music played throughout the show was not your typical generic fare. Brown used music as a sound effect. His organist was warned never to play a recognizable song, or, if he could help it, even an original snatch of melody. The man at the somber organ (a star in his own right) was to play sharp stings—a high musical note struck to emphasize an important piece of dialogue. He also sounded doom chords and cascading crescendos as bridges between scenes.

The host would usher in these proposed tales with dark-humored puns, but the improbable stories themselves were played strictly for thrills. Many times the plots led one to believe that the supernatural was involved. It seemed no other reasoning was possible, but by the time the story reached its conclusion, some kind of logical explanation would prove to take precedence over vampires, ghosts and monsters being the true culprits to the crime. At the conclusion of these unlikely plots, our host would come back to wrap things up with some digging remark. He would then invite the listener to read the latest "Inner

Sanctum" mystery novel published by Simon & Schuster. With that he would gloomily say, "Good niii-iiight … Pleasant dreeeeeaaammmmmmssss" … then the door slammed shut for yet another week.

Both of the male actors in this production (Santos Ortega and Luis Van Rooten) were longtime regulars before the *Inner Sanctum* microphones. Ortega had a most distinguished radio career starring in *The Adventures of Ellery Queen*, *Barrie Craig, Confidential Investigator* and *Bulldog Drummond* and is best remembered as Commissioner Weston on *The Shadow*.

**5.**

disc 3
cass 2
side A/B

**LIGHTS OUT** 12/29/42 "Valse Trieste" by Arch Oboler. Frank Martin (announcer); Arch Oboler (producer/director/host). Starring Dinah Shore (Laura); Gloria Blondell (Dottie Nelson); Lou Merrill (John Boyd); Wally Maher (Jim); Joseph Kearns (Fred).

*Two vacationers sail to an island housing a strange mansion and its equally strange violin-playing owner.*

One of the unsung heroes of radio, Lou Merrill had a twang in his voice that made him sound just a little bit demented. It was for this reason that Arch Oboler frequently used him in his eerie dramas. Merrill was a radio counterpart of Peter Lorre, and knew exactly how to build up suspense with his droll, almost matter-of-fact microphone delivery.

Arch Oboler

Dinah Shore

Arch Oboler was one of those uncharacteristic personalities, who was either liked or disliked, depending, on who you talked to. Evaluation of his contributions to radio ran the gamut from genius to showoff. To some critics, Oboler was radio's top literary genius; to others, he was a flamboyant writer whose style focused on the fulsome. When Oboler took over the helm of *Lights Out* (debut: January 1, 1934) from its creator Wyllis Cooper, he lost no time in establishing himself as the new master of mystery and the macabre. Oboler was not silent in expressing his disappointment with the low standards of radio at that time. In the 1970s, Oboler was quoted as saying: "Radio in those days was an imitation of motion pictures and an echo of the stage. No one had really used it as a theater of the mind. They did not realize that a few words, a sound effect, a bit of music, could transport, in the mind of the listeners, one to any corner of the world and evoke emotions that were deep in the consciousness of the listener."

It was on *Lights Out*, that Oboler developed his much copied stream-of-consciousness technique, as well as his unusual use of sound effects: the sharp terse dialogue and the mastery of precise timing. His own name, indeed, became synonymous with murder, horror and mystery. Oboler equally enjoyed working with budding and established talent, and in this eerie story, future popular singer/entertainer Dinah Shore was his choice.

Dinah Shore first came to radio as a featured vocalist on *The Eddie Cantor Show* in 1939. This popular singer was *Command Performance's* most frequent guest. Dinah Shore's counterpart in this thriller is Gloria Blondell. Blondell was yet another fine radio thespian, who joined a league of the same on such shows as *Escape*, *The Whistler* and *The Adventures of Philip Marlowe*. She was also the curvaceous secretary, Jerry, at the A-1 Detective Agency on the mystery adventure serial, *I Love A Mystery*.

**6.**
disc 1
cass 1
side A/B

**THE MOLLÉ MYSTERY THEATRE** 05/17/46 "Killer Come Back To Me" by Joseph Ruscoll from the story by Ray Bradbury. Alexander Semler (music); Dan Seymour (announcer). Starring Bernard Lenrow (Geoffrey Barnes); Richard Widmark (Johnny Brodman); Alice Reinheart (Julie Parks).

*A gangster's moll trains a small-time hood for the big time.*

Mollé was a brushless shaving cream, almost forgotten today, but the show it sponsored was one of the finest mystery anthologies radio ever had. Expertly produced, and featuring few, if any, big-name stars, it was a favorite of mystery aficionados for years. When this program came to the airwaves (debut: September 7, 1943), it stood as a prototype for other byproducts to come. *The Mollé Mystery Theatre* featured the writings of accomplished authors such as Edgar Allen Poe and Raymond

Ray Bradbury

Chandler, but it also provided opportunities for fledgling writers to have their works produced as well—such was the case with this adapted story.

Ray Bradbury was prolific to say the least, and he was determined at this point in his early career to be a survivor. His intuitive niche in the fields of fantasy and science fiction were on the horizon. He mentions in an introduction to one of his collection of detective/mystery pulps: "My hero and teacher was Leigh Brackett, who in my early years, met with me every Sunday noon at Muscle Beach, in Santa Monica, California. There to read my dreary imitations of her first rate detective tales. Most of my stories were written to please Ms. Leigh, to get an occasional: Well done, or, This is your best yet! I put myself on a regimen of writing one story a week for the rest of my life. I knew that without quantity there could never be any quality."

In this Bradbury opus, up-and-coming actor, Richard Widmark, enacts his words. This radio outing might have prepared Widmark for his future cinema debut in *Kiss of Death* (1947). Giggling maniacally, as he shoves a wheelchair bound woman down a flight of stairs. A far cry from his Broadway role with another "kiss" in the title, *Kiss Them for Me*. This romantic comedy is mentioned at the beginning of the program by Bernard Lenrow, crime fiction connoisseur who introduces the series. Mr. Widmark had made a substantial name for

Richard Widmark

himself on radio before becoming a movie celebrity. Successes included: *Gangbusters, Joyce Jordan, Girl Intern, True Confessions, Big Sister, Suspense,* the one and only *Inner Sanctum Mysteries* and the title role in *Front Page Farrell*.

**7.**

disc 4
cass 3
side A

**MURDER BY EXPERTS** 04/24/50 "Conspiracy" by Harold Swanton, selected by Ursula Curtis. Robert A. Arthur and David Kogan (producers/directors/adapters); Emerson Buckley (music); Richard DuPage (arranger); Walter Schafer (sound effects); Phil Tonkin (announcer); Brett Halliday (host). Starring Lawson Zerbe (Joe Kenicott); Miriam Wolfe (Marilyn); Ronald Dawson; Frank Behrens; Robert Donley.

*A reporter decides to kill his ex-girlfriend during a flood—but he doesn't count on a witness!*

Although *Murder By Experts* ran for just over two years, (debut: June 18, 1949), it offered tales by the leading mystery writers of the day, including: Andrew Evans, Maurice Zimm, Milton Lewis and Joseph Ruscoll. These stories were highly charged plots of crime and passion that conveyed emotion rather than artifice—they were straightforward and honest, revealing a better series than most of its counterparts. *Murder By Experts* utilized alternating hosts for each week's mystery narrative. For one broadcast, it might be the master of the locked room puzzle, John Dickson Carr. The next week (as with this broadcast) it could be the diverse writer, Brett Halliday.

Brett Halliday was born in Chicago in 1904 but was raised in West Texas in the closing days of the old West. A youthful run-in with barbed wire cost him an eye, but it did not prevent him from joining the U.S. Cavalry at age fourteen. After his stint in the service (which included a tour in Mexico with General Pershing), he returned to the United States to finish his education at Tri-State College in Angola, Indiana. He thus began writing full time in 1927. Halliday's real name was Davis Dresser, but it was through a variety of pseudonyms that he eked out a living as a professional writer. The Halliday alias was created to twit an editor who once told Dresser to change a character's name from Halliday because it wasn't "tough enough."

In his early years, Halliday furnished stories to the pulps. One time it might be a western adventure—another—a story of love, romance and the sanctioned sex of the period. His precarious living would change when he published the first experience of Miami private eye, Michael Shayne. This hardboiled creation made Halliday his fortune and spawned a small publishing empire. That fortune spilled into the movie and radio industries too. The reckless redheaded Irishman character came on the film scene first, with *Michael Shayne, Private Detective* in 1940 (based on his novel of that same year, "The Private Practice of Michael Shayne"). Then, his work debuted on radio October 16, 1944.

**8.**

disc 4
cass 3
side A/B

**THE MYSTERIOUS TRAVELER** 07/27/47 "The Man the Insects Hated" by Robert A. Arthur and David Kogan (producers/directors). Carl Caruso (announcer). Starring Maurice Tarplin (The Mysterious Traveler/Mr. Conway); Eric Dressler (Professor John Hanson); Helen Shields (Mary Hanson); Bob Dryden (Martin Andrews/doctor).

*An eccentric professor works to rid the world of insects, while his new assistant "has eyes" for the doctor's wife.*

The sound of a train always seems to convey mystery in some shape or form. This program's beginning (debut: December 5, 1943) had just such a signature—the distant lonely wail of a locomotive, fading in gradually until steel wheels could be heard, clattering on steel rails. Then, the host, who is headlined as a passenger on this phantom train, would invite the listener to join him. This omniscient presenter, once self-described as a former coroner, conveyed a good-natured menace— the same kind of mischievous maliciousness imparted by *The Whistler*, or Raymond, host of the *Inner Sanctum*. Like those characters, The Mysterious Traveler stood outside the stories. He seemed to narrate and comment from inside the soul of his protagonist. The night-riding host was portrayed by a staple of old time radio, Maurice Tarplin.

Tarplin's radio credentials were quite impressive. He was Inspector

Maurice Tarplin

Faraday on the well-known detective series, *Boston Blackie*. He was also on the hitherto mentioned, *The Chase* and *Cloak and Dagger* (based on true adventures of foreign intrigue). He impersonated Winston Churchill on the famous news documentary series, *The March of Time*. *Now Hear This* was another, based on personal experiences of those gallant men and women who embody the traditions of a great service, the U.S. Navy. He was *The Strange Dr. Weird* on the supernatural mystery melodrama of the same name. His résumé also included the science fiction anthology series, *Tales of Tomorrow*, and many soap operas including *Valiant Lady* (he played Barclay, the elderly editor of *The Pine River Review*).

The endings of *The Mysterious Traveler* shows dealt with twisted fate. Many times on the program, the final scream blended into the train's whistle, where the listener would be joined once more with The Mysterious Traveler and his grim comments. Then, realizing time was short, he'd interrupt his own comments by finally adding: "Oh, you have to get off here!…I'm sorry!…I'm sure we'll meet again…I take this same train every week at this same time…"

*The Mysterious Traveler* won mystery-writing Edgars four years in a row (1948 through 1952), an impressive record for any radio series.

The cast of *The Mysterious Traveler*

**9.**

**SUSPENSE** 09/02/42 "The Hitchhiker" by Lucille Fletcher. William Spier (producer); John Dietz (director); Bernard Herrmann (music); Berry Kroeger (announcer). Starring Orson Welles (Ronald Adams).

*Ronald Adams embarks on an unusual journey by car and keeps seeing the same stranger wherever he goes.*

When you think of the best or most well-known radio mystery program, *Suspense* (debut: June 17, 1942) would probably be the first show to come to mind. At its peak, it was one of radio's high-profile shows so it would stand to reason that many of the film stars of the day vied to be a part of this theater of thrills. In its first two years on the air, Orson Welles made five appearances (including four in a row). Welles was a favorite with its producer William Spier and their collaborative efforts included such memorable stories as "The Marvelous Barastro" and "Donovan's Brain" (an unprecedented two-parter). However, it is this strange tale (Welles' first *Suspense* appearance) which is their acknowledged best, then and now. This airing was its command performance, but Welles liked this story so much he would perform it four years later on his own *Mercury Summer Theatre* (June 21, 1946).

The author of this fine script was the very talented Lucille Fletcher. This was her first big break into radio writing, having started out as a

Orson Welles

Agnes Moorehead in *Suspense*'s all-time best show, "Sorry Wrong Number"

typist/secretary at CBS. She herself admitted that this was her favorite composition. Her anecdote on how she came up with the idea was explained, a few years back, on the Chicago radio program, *The When Radio Was Special Edition*. As she told the host, Carl Amari, "My then husband Benny and I were traveling by car from New York to California (just like the character Ronald Adams). We kept seeing a man standing by the side of the road thumbing rides, or we thought it was the same man … and it was very mysterious, to me. We thought, perhaps he was getting rides from cars faster than our car was. So I made a story out of that."

The husband Ms. Fletcher was referring to is the late famous composer, Bernard Herrmann. There was a connection between Herrmann and Welles; Herrmann composed many a musical piece for Welles' *Mercury Theatre on the Air*. There was also a Bernard Herrmann/*Suspense* link as well; Herrmann composed the haunting theme music to the series which waited until the last possible moment to provide its listener with the chilling solution. Fletcher would go on to pen many other episodes of *Suspense*, including its all-time best show, "Sorry Wrong Number" starring Agnes Moorehead. This play (about an invalid, who through a freak telephone connection, overhears a sinister murder plot) was turned into a motion picture of the same name starring Barbara Stanwyck and Burt Lancaster.

A series, some say, is only as good as its director. William Spier, was considered by many to be one of radio's best. Other directing, as well as producing ventures for Spier included: *The Adventures of Sam Spade, Detective*, *The Philip Morris Playhouse* and four hundred performances of *The March of Time*. Charles Vanda was the original producer/director of *Suspense*, but it was William Spier who steered the show toward legendary status. While at the helm, he tried to make the show live up to its motto: "Tales well calculated to keep you in...*Suspense!*"

**10.**

disc 5
cass 4
side A

**TALES OF FATIMA** 05/21/49 "A Much Expected Murder" by Gail Ingram. Harry Ingram (director); Jack Miller (music); Michael Fitzmaurice (announcer). Starring Basil Rathbone (himself); Agnes Young (Lavender); Francis DeSales (Lt. Dennis Farrell); Ralph Bell (Dr. Rand/sergeant).

*A dying man thinks his wife is poisoning him ... can Rathbone save him?*

This series should have been called *The Basil Rathbone Show*, but since its sponsor (Fatima Cigarettes) was footing the bill, it's elementary that they called it *Tales of Fatima*. This series came three years after Rathbone's long run as the foremost detective *Sherlock Holmes* and two years after playing Inspector Burke on the short-lived *Scotland Yard* series. On *Tales of Fatima* (debut: January 8, 1949), Basil Rathbone would find himself in convoluted and contrived murders. He would

Basil Rathbone

always solve them however, with the aid of a metaphysical female who spoke to him in much the same way that the dreamed-up Eugor (Rogue spelled backward) spoke to Dick Powell in *Rogue's Gallery*. The sultry-voiced Fatima was a blatant plug for the sponsor, under the guise of providing clues to the listener and Mr. Rathbone. Rathbone also read the Fatima sales pitches, leading *Radio Life* to complain that the distinguished star "had gone commercial." For a man who supposedly didn't care for radio, except for the paycheck it provided, his rich, cultured voice could be heard all over the airwaves during its golden years.

Rathbone was a guest on virtually every comedy show of the day: *The Jack Benny Program*, *The Bob Hope Show*, *The Fred Allen Show* and *Spotlight Revue with Spike Jones* to name just a few. In the 1940s, he contributed to the war effort by being on the informative patriotic drama, *Ceiling Unlimited*, and then there was his concert reading with the New York Philharmonic on *The(Bell) Telephone Hour*. He was also a guest on game shows including *Information Please*, a quiz program for the intellectual, and *Which Is Which*. Of course his acting talents could also be heard on such dramas as *The Lux Radio Theatre*, *The Electric Theatre*, *Stars Over Hollywood* and *The Screen Guild Theatre*.

Another program Rathbone frequented was an expensive talk show, long before talk was commonplace. This provocative program entitled

*The Circle* featured such stars as Carole Lombard, Cary Grant and Ronald Colman talking about everything from poetry to fur coats. He joined British compatriots like Vivian Leigh, George Sanders, Greer Garson and Laurence Olivier in a June 11, 1939 radio tribute to the King and Queen of England. In the late 1940s, Basil Rathbone completed his California run of the stage play, "The Heiress," giving him a chance to promote Fatima cigarettes. He also got a chance to have his name used for marketing a series of mystery paperback reprints—touting his skill at selecting and solving crimes.

## 11.

disc 6
cass 4
side A/B

**THE WEIRD CIRCLE** 1945 "Dr. Jekyll and Mr. Hyde" adapted from the Robert Louis Stevenson classic story. Starring Berry Kroeger (Dr. Jekyll/Mr. Hyde).

*What happens when a man releases his evil self on the world?*

Lovers of classic mystery tales from the pens of Wilkie Collins, Edgar Allan Poe, Charles Dickens and their contemporaries had a field day listening to these half hour adaptations. Robert Louis Stevenson, the chosen author for program #74 of *The Weird Circle*, proclaimed that he envisioned the entire story of "Dr. Jekyll and Mr. Hyde" in a dream and simply recorded it the way he saw it. Stevenson claimed to be able to dream plots for his stories at will. Although he is primarily known for his adventure novels, "Treasure Island" and "Kidnapped," he did delve

Berry Kroeger

into the field of mystery. He preferred an episodic tale to one with a tightly constructed plot. The creation of a mysterious atmosphere came naturally to him, and he was interested in the borderland where adventure turned into crime. This is evidenced when he collaborated with his stepson (Lloyd Osbourne) for "The Wrong Box" in 1888. His short story, "The Suicide Club," is example of his dabbling with "the thriller." Another enlivened narrative is "The Wrecker" with its full blend of thrills and adventure.

Robert Louis Stevenson was attracted by the romance of mystery, not the science of detection. He was also attracted, like Dr. Henry Jekyll, to the mysterious struggle between good and evil in human nature. Stevenson's wife destroyed his original manuscript of "The Strange Case of Dr. Jekyll and Mr. Hyde" calling it vile and decadent. Consequently, he had to rewrite it by memory making it a masterpiece of literature. Later on, this classic allegory lent itself quite well to stage, screen and radio (first coming before the footlights of the London stage January 29, 1910). J. Comyns Carr was its adapter, with the starring role going to Henry Irving. Then came motion pictures, with the 1920 silent, starring the great profile himself, John Barrymore. It wasn't long after the advent of talking pictures, that director Rouben Mamoulian brought what is considered by many, the best cinematic version to the screen. Premiering in 1932, it provided an Academy Award for its star, Fredric March. Then in 1941, Spencer Tracy (against his wishes), was assigned the dual role.

"The Strange Case of Dr. Jekyll and Mr. Hyde" claims a Freudian dream sequence, an interesting inclusion, given this is how Stevenson came up with his ideas for stories. Throughout the years, a potpourri of versions has come onto the screen—some in a comedy direction (*The Nutty Professor*), others, with a mere kernel of its creator's original conception. Some say you've made your mark in popularity when they make a musical from your story, which is just such the case of "Jekyll and Hyde." Opening in 1990 at the Alley Theatre in Houston, the musical featured Chuck Wagner in the title role(s). Frank Wildhorn provided the music, with lyrics by Leslie Bricusse—who also furnished lyrics for another famous fictional character's musical venue—*Sherlock Holmes*.

**12.**

disc 6
cass 4
side B

**THE WHISTLER** 08/28/49 "The Eager Pigeon" by Joel Malone and Adrian Gendot. George W. Allen (producer); Sterling Tracy (director); Wilbur Hatch (music); Marvin Miller (announcer). Starring Bill Forman (The Whistler); Jack Webb (Danny Thorpe); Kaye Brinker (Monica Scott); Willis Bouchey (butler/Sergeant Rickels).

*A man down on his luck accepts an offer from a femme fatale that could mean disaster.*

Bill Forman

Lobby card for the first of Columbia's noir films based on CBS's *The Whistler*

The three-hour time difference between the East and West Coasts led to much experimentation to fill open timeslots. *The Whistler* became a West Coast favorite and was broadcast almost exclusively in that region (debut: May 16, 1942). It ran for thirteen years, which was a lucky number for this popular crime show. Its signature beginning ranks up there as one of radio's greatest. The program opened with echoing footsteps and a lingering eerie whistle. It's that haunting whistle that was destined to become one of the all-time remembered themes. It consisted of an ascending series of wailing notes, followed by the soulful whistling of the title character. Later, as with this broadcast, banal lyrics were added, promoting its sponsor, the Signal Oil company. This type of whistling was extremely difficult for most whistlers to master. The only person who was consistently able to whistle the two-octave theme music (composed by Wilbur Hatch) was a woman by the name of Dorothy Roberts. She performed the tricky whistling on the program for most of the series' run.

After the whistled tune, the orchestra would join in, followed by the voice of The Whistler himself: "I am the Whistler, and I know many things, for I walk by night. I know many strange tales hidden in the hearts of men and women who have stepped into the shadows. Yes, I know the nameless terrors of which they dare not speak." He would proceed to tell stories of the everyday gone amiss—of men and

Jack Webb

women driven to murder and then being tripped up in a cunning double twist. All the while, the voice of The Whistler would interject his fateful malevolence as the story unfolded. This omniscient storytelling format was also used on *The Mysterious Traveler* and in the early years of *The Shadow*.

Some of the best radio thespians in the business worked on *The Whistler*, and unlike *Suspense*, policy dictated their names be mentioned at the end of the program. Radio actors and actresses such as William Conrad, Betty Lou Gerson, Joan Banks and Gerald Mohr all played an important part in the success of *The Whistler*. The star of this broadcast, Jack Webb, can also be listed among the rank and file.

Webb had taken part in every aspect of old time radio. His resonant voice could be heard on *Pat Novak, For Hire*; *Jeff Regan, Investigator*; *Johnny Modero: Pier 23* and *Pete Kelly's Blues*. The hard-edged quips and caustic one-liners were the staple dialogue on these hard-boilers. But the show that really brought his name to prominence was the one and only *Dragnet*—the hallmark police drama that aimed for realism.

Listeners on the East Coast got a few opportunities to hear *The Whistler* when it stretched cross-country, and later, when it went into syndication. Fondly remembered to this day, this brings our collection to a close.

# Sources for the Information in This Booklet

Amari, Carl. *The When Radio Was Special Edition*. Radio Spirits, Inc., 1998.

Bradbury, Ray. *A Memory of Murder*. Dell Publishing, 1984.

DeAndrea, William L. *Encyclopedia Mysteriosa—A Comprehensive Guide to the Art of Detection in Print, Film, Radio, and Television.* Prentice Hall General Reference, 1994.

Dunning, John. On the Air—*The Encyclopedia of Old Time Radio*. Oxford University Press, 1998.

Harmon, Jim. *The Great Radio Heroes*. Doubleday & Co., 1967.

Lackmann, Ron. *Same Time… Same Station - An A-Z Guide To Radio From Jack Benny To Howard Stern.* Facts on File Inc., 1996.

MacDonald, Fred J. *Don't Touch That Dial - Radio Programming in American Life from 1920 to 1960*. Nelson Hall, 1979.

Maltin, Leonard. *Movie and Video Guide*. Signet, 1998.

Symons, Julian. *Bloody Murder*. Penguin Books Ltd., 1972.

# Credits

**Radio Spirits**
Carl Amari, Executive Producer
Vincent Amari, Assistant
Christine Birkett, Graphic Designer
Joel Bogart, Illustrator
Jerry Burling, Technical Support/Equipment Maintenance
David Kogan, Author (foreword)
Chris Lembesis, Audio Restoration Engineer
Dennis Levin, Licensing Director
William Nadel, Research Assistant
Lawrence Nepodahl, Author
Christina Vrba, Project Manager
Roger Wolski, Audio Restoration/Mastering Engineer

**Smithsonian Institution**
Peter Reid, Director, Smithsonian Product Development and Licensing

## About the Author

Lawrence Nepodahl has worn many (deerstalker) hats in his life. He's a mystery/detective historian, an audio/visual technician at Northern Illinois University, an actor and even a Sherlockian. He has taken part in a few radio recreations of the man from 221-B Baker Street. He worked behind the microphone for many years in Illinois and throughout South Dakota, the state of his ancestors. He has also been a guest many times on the radio program, *The When Radio Was Special Edition.*